Stephen, King's Troubled Ass

A Novelette

Atit Humagain

This is a work of fiction. Names, characters, businesses, places, events, locales, and incidents are either the products of the author's imagination or used in a fictitious manner. Any resemblance to actual persons, living or dead, or actual events is purely coincidental.

Contents

CHAPTER 1

"It's time, send message to the King," said Antonius, giving last touch to the gallows. Octavius raised his head to the whimpering sounds and took a brief look on three gallows set alongside each other. He turned and carefully stepped down the wooden platform covered in snow, and headed towards the throne-hall. While walking on the wet stone paved pathway, Octavius pondered about other options to the death penalty he would opt, if he were the King. A tall guard hidden inside steel armor, with a sword length of Octavius himself, blocked the entrance to the hall.

"Message for the King," said Octavius.

"Let him in." A soft but commanding sound came through the half-open door. The guard took a step sideways, making way for Octavius. He walked in as his steps echoed through the empty hall. There sat the King on the throne with teardrops hanging on his chin, like water drops on a freshly melting ice.

"It's time, your majesty," said Octavius. The King nodded without an eye contact, as Octavius slowly turned and exited the hall.

CHAPTER 2

The Sare Castel City was going through a snow blizzard. The constant sound of blowing wind was deafening. Snow covered the city knee deep. Visibility was low and people had covered themselves in furry clothes. In a corner of the city lived a winemaker named Otto. It was not one of the biggest business of the area but was enough to feed his pregnant wife and two children. But one day, they banned the wine making business in the city, on direct order from the King.

"Where are you going?" asked Otto's wife.

"At the glassmaker's place," replied Otto.

"I hope you are not sneaking out wine for your friends again."

"Of course not, it's banned remember?"

"What's on that bag then?" she asked with a smile.

He kissed her on the forehead and said, "I will be back before the dinner." With a bag that made the sound of bottles clinking every time moved, he walked towards the frozen lake.

On the other part of the city lived Rhodes, a pick pocketer. He always used his thin and short physique for advantage whenever needed. Imprisoned twice already, he was warned to be exiled if caught doing anything against the law. The crimes committed were not severe enough to get hanged.

"Come on, man, it's worth three hundred monedas," said Rhodes, with a shiny metal goblet in his hand.

"I cannot give you more than twenty. And I don't know where you stole it from."

"Hey watch it alright. This is my family's property. My grandfather drank wine on this goblet on a meeting with King, once. And before dying, he passed it to me."

"Yeah sure."

"So you are not giving me three hundred monedas for it?"

"No."

"Twenty it is then."

He handed the goblet and exited the pawnshop with twenty monedas. He was late already as he headed towards the frozen lake.

In the northern part of the Sare Castel City was an enormous lake named Degerat Lake. It froze during most part of the year. When Rhodes arrived on the bank of the lake, there was a man wrapped in furry clothes sitting on a log. Rhodes walked near, but when the person looked back, Rhodes found out it was not the person he was hoping to see. He sat on the back, a few feet away from the stranger, waiting.

A man in a horse, with a hat and leather shoe with spur, wrapped in deerskin, approached, making his way through the knee deep snow.

"Hey Rhodes," said the man, and walked towards another. "So, Otto, how many bottles did you bring?"

"I said two, Lazarus, and I brought two only," replied Otto.

Lazarus opened a bottle and sat near Otto. After taking a sip, he said, "Hey Rhodes, come here, I did not know you were the shy kind."

Rhodes walked towards them and sat next to Lazarus. "Can I take a sip or two?" said Rhodes.

"Now there is the Rhodes I know," said Lazarus, and handed the bottle, laughing.

Taking a sip, Rhodes said, "Where did you get it, it's banned in all areas right?"

Lazarus laughed once again, whereas Otto smiled. "I'm sorry, I forgot to introduce you guys. Rhodes, meet Otto. Otto, meet Rhodes."

They smiled and shook hands.

"Where did you get the wine from?" asked Rhodes to Otto.

"He is a winemaker. Or should I say *he was a wine maker*?" added Lazarus.

The face of Otto narrowed. "You said there would be four of us," he said.

"Yes, he will be here soon. He must be on his way," replied Lazarus.

CHAPTER 3

Cicero answered the door after a few knocks.

"You little piece of shit," said Lazarus, with a smile.

"Brother," said Cicero, as he approached Lazarus for a hug.

"It's been long, hasn't it?" said Lazarus, as he took off his furry coat covered in snow.

"Well, you barely get time from your travel," said Cicero, as he led Lazarus to a table near the fire.

"And your job in the King's castle, does that give you time?" said Lazarus, followed by a wink.

"Come sit, I have a surprise for you?"

"Surprise?"

A woman appeared through a wooden door with two glasses of home-made rice beer. Lazarus had never seen the woman before.

"Meet my wife," said Cicero with a grin.

"No freakin' way." The eyes of Lazarus suddenly widened.

Cicero's wife shied away and locked herself inside the room she earlier came out of.

"It just happened in a hurry."

"Congratulations you turd," said Lazarus, and gulped down the rice beer. "It tastes like shit," he added, as skin on his nose folded with disgust.

"Since the ban, drinking wine has been no less than a fantasy," said Cicero. "Actually, I had something to discuss you with."

"What is it?"

Cicero gestured Lazarus to listen closely as he whispered, leaning forward, "I have a plan. A big, very big plan."

"I'm listening."

"But it needs four men. We need two more."

"What is the plan?" asked Lazarus.

"Steal something from the castle that will set our life."

"Set our life?"

"Yes brother, no more rice beer, no more job in the castle, no fighting for a couple of bites. And you won't have to travel around collecting trash and sell it for a tiny margin."

"I love traveling. But go on," said Lazarus, with his eyes locked on Cicero.

"There is a special chamber in the castle where King keeps his most valuable belongings."

"But it's the King's castle, how can we pull this off?"

"Brother, I work in the castle. I've worked things out. You just find two guys for me."

"Don't you worry about that. Meet me by the frozen lake tomorrow afternoon. You will have two perfect guys for the mission. And you know what, I will make sure you get a bottle of finest wine Sare Castel have ever tasted."

CHAPTER 4

Rhodes and Otto were walking through a trail between piles of snow on either side, where branches of trees were white, covered in snow. Otto's leg was burning, but there was no option other than to walk as fast as they could, if not run. Rhodes held to the lead of the ass up front, showing way, whereas Otto gave a hand to the two giant vessels, tied on each side of the ass. The speed by which they previously walked had slowed down. Even the ass sauntered.

"Do you think this ass is sick?" asked Otto to Rhodes.

"What made you think that?"

"The vessels almost fell twice because of the disbalance."

"It's an ass. What does it know about balancing things?"

"They carry things all the time, things tied in balance should remain in balance throughout the journey," replied Otto.

"Maybe it is hungry or tired."

"Could be."

Suddenly, the ass stopped. Rhodes pulled the lead and the ass hee-hawed.

"Walk you stupid ass," yelled Rhodes.

"Let me push from behind," said Otto, and gave it a push.

The ass kicked Otto with one of its back legs on his treasure. Otto fell on the ground, grabbing his assets as his eyes filled with tears. He could hardly breathe. After catching a breath, Otto said, "I'm going to kill this thing."

"Move, you idiot," yelled Rhodes, and pulled the rope even harder.

The ass slid a little with the force but was unwilling to walk. When Otto finally got up and joined Rhodes in the front, the ass turned its head towards lower floor of a house on the side. It was an eatery.

"I think it's hungry or thirsty, maybe tired. Should we take a break?" asked Otto.

"We have walked for a couple of hours now. A few minutes' break should be safe."

After taking the vessels off the ass, Otto and Rhodes sat on a table outside whereas they left the donkey to munch on grass that was covered in snow. The ass stood staring at them. When ordered cheese with nuts and mushroom arrived, the ass ran and munched on one of the plates. Rhodes tried his best to push the ass away from the plate but was unsuccessful. In no time, the plate was empty.

"Stupid jackass," yelled Rhodes on ass' face.

With a cheeky smile, Otto said, "Let's share my plate."

The ass kept staring at Rhodes, showing two of its front teeth as if it was teasing him. Rhodes slid the plate away from the ass to the other side of the table as he and Otto finished the food in a hurry.

"Isn't this thing thirsty?" asked Otto, as Rhodes gulped water from the jug.

"It would be kicking us now for the jug if it was thirsty. I heard they last three days after drinking."

Rhodes helped Otto to load the vessels on to the ass before taking the lead.

"Put the tongue inside your mouth, you stupid ass," yelled Rhodes. The ass kept showing its teeth with its tongue hanging on the side. "Did you notice, earlier when it hee-hawed, the sound was more like a baby screaming."

Otto laughed and replied, "This ass is something, isn't it?"

They walked for a few hours more. Otto and Rhodes were dragging themselves whereas the ass anchored its leg on the ground after every ten minutes of walk.

"Stop," yelled someone in a horse from a distance. They turned behind, but the man was too far to recognize the identity. As the man neared, the sound of moving metal armor became louder. "Stop right there."

The Royal badge welded to his metal armor was enough for Rhodes and Otto to know he was a King's guard. He got off his horse and took his shiny sword off his scabbard.

"I think there has been a mistake, sir," said

Rhodes, in an innocent voice.

"Is that so?" The guard walked around the ass and added, "And these vessels belong to you people?"

"Yes sir, me and my brother were taking it to the market, to sell you know," said Rhodes, but this time with a shaky voice.

"We will know everything when we reach the castle. Now turn around."

"Sir, we just came through that way. There has been a mist…"

"Shut your bloody mouth and turn around," yelled the guard, placing the edge of his sword on Rhodes neck.

Otto grabbed the rope and turned the ass around in a hurry. "We will do as you say sir, forgive him," said Otto.

"You sound like a wise man. Before we head back, I need to tie your hands."

With wrists of Rhodes and Otto tied together, the guard also tied the ass' lead on Otto's wrist. They walked with the ass up front, whereas the guard rode on a horse behind them. It was a long journey to the castle, and it was about to be dark.

"Can't you guys walk any faster?" asked the guard. He raised the leg from the saddle and kicked the ass on its behind. The ass turned in anger, but was too tired to react.

"We have walked all day sir, we are worn out," replied Otto.

"We might need a place to spend the night then."

They reached the place where they ate earlier. The guard tied Rhodes and Otto's hand in a small tree and walked in to inquire of a room to stay.

"We will spend the night here," yelled the guard from a distance as he walked near to untie them. "We will head towards the castle first thing in the morning."

They entered a room full of haystacks and no furniture. It was more of a stable than a room.

"So no bed. On top of a haystack it is," said the guard.

The guard untied their hands and helped to take the vessels off the ass' back. They tied the ass to a bamboo pole and spread the haystack in a shape of a bed. After everything was ready, the guard tied their arms again.

"Lots of food for the ass here," said the guard.

"Sir, this ass does not eat hay, it likes cheese with nuts and mushroom," added Rhodes, in a soft voice.

"What?" said the guard, with a smile, as he approached the makeshift bed.

The guard fell asleep in no time, whereas Otto and Rhodes barely closed their eyes. The ass was rounding the poll. Rhodes signaled Otto to approach the ass. He dragged himself and placed his tied wrist in front of the ass and the ass looked back, confused. Rhodes bit the rope tied to his wrist, signaling the ass to do the same. When the ass chewed off the ropes from Otto and Rhodes hand, they carefully untied the ass and exited the room without making a sound. Rhodes and Otto went back in to pick the vessels. They tied the vessels on back of the ass once again. After walking a few feet away from the eatery, they all ran as fast as they could.

"That was close, wasn't it," said Otto, in a shaky voice, followed by a grin.

Rhodes smiled and gave Otto a side hug. "Yep, that's it. The King knows now and probably the whole Sare Castel. We need an alternative route and a different plan," added Rhodes, catching his breath. This time they walked in a different direction, unaware where it would lead them.

CHAPTER 5

"So this is it, guys. There might not be a turning back after we enter that gate," said Lazarus. With a Wagon full of potatoes, Otto, Rhodes and Lazarus stared at the King's Castle from a distance. The Castle made of enormous blocks of stone was in a tiny hill surrounded by a jungle, covered in snow. With the chilly breeze, as the time ticked, Otto's leg shook and his face turned red.

"How are you feeling, Rhodes?" asked Lazarus.

"Let's do it."

"Yes, it's time," said Lazarus, signaling Otto to be ready as well.

Lazarus took control of the wagon in the wagoner's position. Whereas, Rhodes and Otto hid along the potato sacks, under a cover, on the back of the wagon. Lazarus drove uphill on a road that ran through the jungle. They reached the gate of the King's castle when the sun began hiding under the horizon.

"Stop," said a guard on the gate. Two guards walked to the wagon, one of which was Cicero. The other guard took a step to see what was loaded and covered in the wagon. Cicero stopped him, blocking his way with his hand.

"I will check this one," said Cicero.

He walked on the behind and lifted the cover to take a glance. Rhodes winked at Cicero whereas Otto, although red faced, could not help but smile.

"What is in it?" asked the other guard.

"Nothing. Just a bunch of spuds. Good to go."

The other guard signaled to open the gate, and Lazarus drove the Wagon inside the castle.

"This is it. My shift is over," said Cicero and headed inside the castle.

Lazarus stopped the Wagon near the castle's kitchen, alongside other food Wagons. He looked around. By taking advantage of the approaching darkness, he walked behind and hid under the cover along with Otto and Rhodes. The space was tight, but they adjusted along the potato sacks. And they still needed space for one more person.

"So when you will be rich, which is tomorrow, what will you do?" asked Lazarus to Otto.

"I don't know. Buy nice things for wife and kids, buy a better place to live in. Maybe I will move to a place where winemakers need not worry about their business."

"Sounds good. Your dream might come true in next twenty-four hours. Or maybe you will get caught and hang cold on one of King's Gallows," joked Lazarus, followed by a laughter.

Otto did not react, so Lazarus asked the same question to Rhodes.

"I'm planning to kill all three of you and take everything with me," replied Rhodes.

Otto and Rhodes could hear the sound of Lazarus swallowing spit. There was silence for a short time before Rhodes could no longer hold the laughter.

"I was just kidding, Lazar," said Rhodes.

"Lazar huh, is that your nickname?" asked Otto.

"Few people call me by that name."

Suddenly someone lifted the cover. The snow had started to fall and there stood a dark figure.

"I could hear you guys from ten passus away. People passing by could easily hear you. How stupid could you be?"

"Stop yelling Cicero, or they will definitely hear us," said Lazarus.

"Move," said Cicero, and squeezed himself into the tight space between the potato sacks. "Everybody will whisper from now on," he added.

"It's already getting harder to breathe. How will we spend so many hours under this cover?" asked Otto.

"Well, we don't have much choice now, do we?" said Cicero.

"You are covered in snow. Your cold shoulder is touching my cheek," said Rhodes.

"Well, we don't have much choice in that regard either, do we?" replied Cicero.

Everybody laughed with their mouth closed with a failed attempt to control the sound. But the snow blizzard was making enough sound now to cover their voice. Hours passed by as all three, except Otto, fell asleep. Otto's eyes wanted rest, but all the thoughts and worries kept him awake.

"Lazarus, wake up," whispered Otto, shaking him gently. Lazarus grabbed Otto by his throat, half asleep. "It's me, what are you doing?" yelled Otto.

"Shush..." said Rhodes as he and Cicero woke as well.

"Why are you guys yelling, you want to get us all killed?" whispered Rhodes.

"Don't mind him, he is a cranky sleeper," said Cicero, as Lazarus came to sense.

"I think it's time," said Otto, rubbing his throat.

Cicero peeped out, raising the cover. The blizzard had not stopped. "Come on," he said.

All of them got off the wagon one by one. Cicero led in the darkness along with the chilly wind, and the others followed. With the map of every corner of the castle imprinted on his brain, he could walk around the castle even with his eyes closed. Cicero led them to the armor storage chamber.

"Why nobody guards this chamber?" asked Otto.

"Look at these craps nicely. They are either broken or dented. These are trash," replied Cicero.

Rhodes, Otto and Lazarus made best use of what they found in the chamber, full of broken gears.

"Now we're talking. I would not know a difference between other guards and you guys," said Cicero. "Except you Rhodes. You're too skinny. You look like a shirt on a hanger," added Cicero. Everybody laughed, except Rhodes.

"Don't we need a sword?" asked Otto.

"Take one scabbard each from there," said Cicero, pointing to a corner.

Otto jumped to the corner and grabbed three. "These are incredibly light," he said.

"That's because it has sword made of wood in it. Now let's get on our way."

They could finally walk in the light, not worrying about other guards. Cicero led the way once again. They climbed a round-staircase, made of stone blocks, that led to the second floor of the castle.

"Wow, look at that statue," said Otto, pointing to an enormous statue of the King, that was in the middle of the round-staircase. "I've never seen anything so big. And he has a dog by his side," he added.

"It is a weird-looking dog," added Rhodes.

Rhodes and Otto were having a hard time walking in the heavy gears, whereas Lazarus walked with comfort.

"Can you guys at least act like a guard?" said Cicero.

"Cicero, is that you?" A sound echoed throughout the staircase.

Cicero turned around, looked everywhere, but saw no one. "Go go… I will meet you guys ahead," Cicero whispered and then yelled, "Who is it?"

A man appeared from the passageway below and stood near the staircase. "Isn't your shift over? Why aren't you home?" he asked.

"Yes, General, I was about to head home."

"What are you doing wandering around the castle at this hour?"

"I needed to see Ned, to inquire about the

available horses, General."

"Recently married, wife alone at home. Get home already," he said laughing, and walked back into the passage he came out of.

Taking a deep breath, he rushed to catch up with the others. They were hiding behind a giant pillar, waiting for him.

"Who was it?" asked Otto whispering.

"It was the General, it's fine, let's move ahead. And this time, we walk in a line."

They tried to walk as if they were in a parade.

"Guards ahead, guards ahead," whispered Rhodes.

"Shut up and walk confidently," Cicero whispered back.

The guards stared as they walked.

"Somebody has been skipping the dinner," said a guard, looking at Rhodes.

"And lunch and breakfast," added another guard, as they all laughed.

Rhodes gave a side look with a red face and kept walking ahead.

"How did he even qualify for the post?" whispered a guard to another.

"Don't listen to them, Rhodes," said Otto.

After walking for a few minutes, they reached a chamber. The door was locked and there were no guards outside.

"Let me remind you, a hundred passus to the right, there is King's chamber, full of guards. We need to be quiet and careful," said Cicero.

Cicero took out a big iron key, hidden inside his leather boot, and unlocked the door. He slowly pushed the door as Otto grabbed a thick beeswax candle from a pit, used in lighting up the passage, and entered the chamber. Cicero closed the door without making a sound. The view they saw inside was unexpected.

"Where are all the golds and silver and whatever that makes me rich? What is this?" said Lazarus.

There was a king-size bed, a big candle chandelier hanging on the roof, a fine carpet on the floor, two giant vessels besides the bed and lots of fruits on the table. Otto blew the candle he held as the chamber was well lit already. There was a small door on the right.

"Did we mistakenly entered the King's chamber?" asked Otto.

"No, it's not the King's chamber," replied Cicero.

"What is it then?"

"I don't know. We don't have much time, search every corner," said Cicero.

They searched under the bed, behind the table and every other corner, but found nothing valuable.

Rhodes noticed something on the far corner, "Could the treasure be behind that small door?" he asked.

Suddenly the small door opened. All four took their sword out their scabbard, three of them made of wood. An ass pushed through the door and froze as he rolled his eyes towards all four of them. They rushed towards the small door, hoping there was something valuable inside. The foul smell of urine pushed them right back. They closed the door and looked on each other's face. They sat on the carpet forming a circle with the ass in the middle.

"It's the vessel. It is the only thing possible," said Lazarus.

"He is right. Maybe it's made of some valuable material or something," said Otto.

"Have you seen the size of that thing? How will we carry it out?"

They thought for a while, staring at the ass that stood in the middle.

"The ass," said Otto, as his face glowed.

"Yeah, we can use the ass," said Rhodes.

"But how did the ass get inside the chamber? It was locked from the outside," asked Otto.

"We will have plenty of time to think once we get out of here. Let's get it done first," said Cicero.

They snatched the rope that held the curtain and tied the vessels on the back of the ass. They also used the rope to make a lead for the ass and covered it with the curtain.

"What will we say when the guards ask what it is?" asked Otto.

"A baby horse maybe," said Lazarus, followed by a laughter.

"We just need to reach the back gate I showed earlier, then it's an easy way out through the jungle," said Cicero. "We need someone who can hold the vessels in place and stop it from sliding down the ass' back. I will stay behind, one of you take the lead," he added.

"Otto and I will take the lead, you guys make sure the vessels stay on place," said Rhodes.

Rhodes opened the door slowly and looked to either side. It was clear, so he and Otto stepped out of the chamber and pulled the ass out slowly.

Rhodes then gave a look to Otto and nodded.

"What is that?" said Otto pointing inside the chamber through the door.

Cicero and Lazarus, who were still inside the chamber, ready to step out, turned back to see what it was. Otto kicked Lazarus whereas Rhodes kicked Cicero. They fell on their back, on the floor, inside the chamber. Rhodes locked the door with help of the key Cicero earlier left on the keyhole.

CHAPTER 6

Sun had risen above the horizon and they were off the route they planned to escape the Sare Castel. Walking through a small pathway covered in snow, Otto could not help worrying about his wife and the children. What would he be without his family? What would be the point of everything he did, if his family was not with him to share the joy? How much could he trust Rhodes on this journey?

"What is the biggest crime you ever committed?" asked Otto.

"Biggest Crime?"

"Yes."

"That's personal, something I'm not comfortable sharing with."

Otto sensed something was not right. Why was Rhodes trying to avoid answering this question?

He could be a murderer. It could be a matter of time before Rhodes did something bad to him.

"I am a winemaker with a clean past. I shared all the information without hesitation," said Otto.

"Yeah, I know you did."

"And what's wrong with you doing the same?"

"Why is it important?"

"I left my pregnant wife and children for this, I'm walking with all my trust on you. Don't you think I should know you better?"

"If it is that important, I will tell, it's not a big thing."

"Yeah, it's important."

"I've put a knife on a man's chest."

"You murdered someone?"

"I did not say he died."

Otto did not say a word further. He had left his family in danger, kicked someone and locked him in the castle, and was walking with a couple of vessels and an ass with a potential murderer. He trusted a criminal to sell the vessels and split the money. The ass suddenly stopped walking, anchoring his legs to the ground. They had reached a settlement that looked more like a marketplace. "Now what's wrong with him," said Rhodes.

"Maybe it is hungry."

"Are you hungry?" asked Rhodes to Otto.

"I am."

They looked for an eatery with tables outside. After finding one, they took the vessels off the ass. Rhodes went in and ordered the food while Rhodes sat on a table outside.

"What did you order?" asked Otto when Rhodes returned.

26

"The same. Cheese with nuts and mushroom."

"Is that your favorite dish?"

"Sort of." Rhodes then turned towards the ass and added, "Wait a minute." He went inside once again and came back.

"You forgot something inside?" asked Otto.

"No. Actually, I previously ordered two plates, but I went back to add one more."

Otto could not help but laugh. While Otto and Rhodes had occasional chats as they rested their legs, the ass slowly walked behind the restaurant. Otto noticed but was too tired to stand up and look. After a few minutes, Otto could not help but inquire whether the ass had escaped.

"We forgot to tie the ass, I will bring him back," said Otto and walked to the direction the ass went.

Otto walked over and looked around but could not see the ass. Suddenly somebody pushed a door open near him. It was the door of a small compartment used as a toilet. The ass came out of it. The ass and Otto stood still as they looked on each other's eyes in silence. Otto walked back to the table, and the ass followed. Otto sat back in his seat, scratching his head.

"You forgot to tie the ass once again," said Rhodes.

"It's fine. You ordered three plates, right? It's time to eat anyway," replied Otto.

When the food arrived, Rhodes slid a plate on the edge of the table. The ass walked to the table and ate along with Otto and Rhodes. When Otto poured water off the jug on to a glass, the ass kept staring.

"I think the ass is thirsty," said Rhodes.

"Huh?"

"The ass. It's staring at you pouring the water." Rhodes grabbed a jug and poured water on the floor. The ass backed a little, saving himself from the water drops. "I will never understand this stupid animal," added Rhodes.

Otto stood and walked to the ass. He joined his hands in shape of a bowl in front of ass' face and said, "Can you help pour the water on to my hand?"

Rhodes did as asked. When he poured the water, the ass drank from Otto's hand. They poured a couple of jugs and the ass drank them all.

"Wow, that's one picky, high fashioned ass," said Rhodes.

Otto smiled, and they got ready for their travel. After walking a few hours, the tiredness and lack of sleep started getting into them. The ass just sat down and refused to walk further. Otto and Rhodes were sleepy and tired too.

"Come on, ass, we will rest as soon as we find a place," said Otto and tried his best to pull the ass. But the ass had made its mind. It refused to stand up.

Rhodes looked around and said, "I have an idea." In a distance, between the trees and snow filled fields, he walked towards an elevation. It had a tree and a small flat ground good enough for camping. "You look after the ass for a while."

"Where are you going?" asked Otto, but did not get a reply.

Rhodes walked to the place and cleared the snow with the help of his feet and the fallen branches of the tree. He then gathered wood and started a fire. Otto and the ass sat in a distance watching him. "Come on," yelled Rhodes.

The ass stood up and walked towards the fire. Otto smiled and followed the ass. Rhodes took off the leather sheet he had used to cover himself from snow and laid it on the ground. They took off the vessels off the ass and placed it behind the tree, and tied the ass as well. Otto took off his leather sheet too. Rhodes and he sat near the fire on one sheet while using other as a blanket. They chatted for a few hours before they noticed something.

"Is the ass shaking?" asked Rhodes.

"Yeah, I think it is cold."

Otto stood up, untied the ass and led it to the sheet near the fire. The ass sat in the middle. The ass got warmth from Rhodes and Otto as well as the fire blazing in front of them. Since it was still shaking, Otto hugged the ass sideways with one arm wrapped to it. Rhodes did not look comfortable with it, but Otto did not care. The ass stopped shaking after a while. The three sat in front of the fire under the tree as they fell asleep on top of each other.

When Otto woke up, Rhodes was yelling, "You stupid ass."

"What happened?" asked Otto.

"He bathe me in his droll."

Otto laughed and said, "Come on, we need to move."

It was evening, and there was a light snowfall. They covered the remain of the fire with snow, loaded the vessels and got on their way. While Rhodes and Otto covered themselves in the leather sheet, the ass walked with no cover from the snow.

Otto observed the ass. It was not shaking and was walking in comfort. Donkey's hair is supposed to keep them warm. Why didn't it work earlier?

"Whoa, look at that?" said Rhodes, as his eyes widened.

Up ahead, there was a huge line of horses, donkeys, men and cows. It was as long as their eyes could see.

"They are Migratie Banda," said Otto.

"Migratie Banda?"

"Yes, they travel for weeks, sometimes even months. They migrate and trade."

"We can follow them then. They must be heading to a bigger market where we can sell these vessels," said Rhodes.

"That's a fantastic idea."

The Migratie Banda walked ahead whereas they followed. After a few hours they were behind the line as if they were part of the Migratie Banda. The last one in the line was walking alongside a cow. When he noticed two people and an ass walking behind him, he turned around and gave a friendly smile.

"Where are you heading?" asked Otto to the man.

"To the Sare Tarm," he said.

"Is there a market in Sare Tarm?" asked Otto.

"A very big market. People from all around go there for trade."

"Ask him how far it is," whispered Rhodes in Otto's ear.

"How far is the Sare Tarm from here?" asked Otto to the man.

"Three."

"Three? Three days of travel?"

"Three months," replied the man.

It shocked them. They were not prepared for a three-months travel. And they did not even know if there would be any buyer who would give them the right price for the vessels. They hardly knew the value of the vessels.

"Are you looking to sell the ass?" asked the man.

"How much would you pay for it?" asked Rhodes.

The man left the cow and approached the ass. The ass brayed and kicked the man.

"Okay, that's enough. The ass is not for sale. How much would you pay for the vessels?" asked Otto.

"Vessels?"

"Yes, these vessels."

"Why would I buy vessels?"

"You don't understand, these are not ordinary vessels. These are valuable."

"How so?" asked the man.

"Well, these vessels are from…"

"From his own home," added Rhodes, shutting Otto's mouth.

"You guys are strange," said the man and joined the line once again.

Rhodes and Otto slowed the pace to maintain a distance from the Migratie Banda.

"Have you lost your mind? If you tell every stranger we meet that these vessels were stolen from the King's castle, we will be dead in no time," said Rhodes.

"I'm sorry, I did not think it through," said Otto.

Up ahead, the Migratie Banda walked through a flat land, clearing the snow.

"It is the Alb-Rau river ahead," said Otto.

"I don't see no river."

"It is frozen and covered in snow."

"Wow, it's wide. Must be huge," said Rhodes.

"It is wide, but the depth is no more than waist deep."

"I hope it's safe to walk on it."

"It normally is, but as the huge line of Migratie Banda walked over it before us, it might crack before we walk on it."

"What?" said Rhodes as his face turned red.

Otto laughed and said, "Relax, I'm just kidding."

Darkness had almost approached and the distance between Migratie Banda and them had widened, although within sight. They had crossed the river, and it was time for Otto and Rhodes to do the same. The ass disagreed to walk on the frozen river at first, but after Otto slowly walked and stood on it, the ass finally stepped on it too. The darkness was approaching with a few minutes of light left. Rhodes and Otto were walking ahead chatting, whereas the ass was right behind them. As soon as Otto and Rhodes stepped on the ground on the other side, the ice floor behind them cracked. The ass fell in the river along with the vessels. The ass cried loud and harsh. Otto and Rhodes looked at each other's face.

"Start a fire," yelled Otto, then threw his leather sheet and jumped into the water.

Rhodes gathered every bit of wood he could and did his best to start a fire. Otto, soaked wet in freezing water, pushed the ass as hard as he could to get it off the water. The weight of the vessels was not helping, so he untied the vessels off the ass' back and gave a hard push. Rhodes was finally successful to start the fire. He then dragged a big log covered in snow into the fire, opened his clothes and jumped right in. They were finally able to push the ass off the water. The ass walked and sat on the ground near the fire, shaking. Rhodes and Otto carried the vessels off the water and climbed back. All three sat near the fire, shaking. Otto and Rhodes wanted to speak, the donkey wanted to hee-haw, but their skin was almost frozen and they were shaking uncontrollably. Wrapped in the leather sheet, all three stood by the fire, hugging each other as the night approached.

CHAPTER 7

"Hey Rhodes, come here, I did not know you were the shy kind," said Lazarus.

Rhodes was always shy around new faces. Lazarus talking as if he knew Rhodes very well, and calling him as if he was a puppy, did not impress Rhodes. Lazarus and the new guy were talking like best friends, and barging into the conversation was out of Rhodes' personality. How could he make himself comfortable around them?

"Can I take a sip or two?" said Rhodes, trying his best to hide the awkwardness.

"Now there is the Rhodes I know," said Lazarus, and handed the bottle.

Why does this Otto guy have two bottles of wine? Could he be a smuggler or perhaps a thief? It takes guts to walk around carrying wine bottles, especially in a place where the punishment could be a death sentence. He had to know. Taking a sip, Rhodes said, "Where did you get it, it's banned in all areas right?"

Lazarus laughed, and Otto smiled. "I'm sorry, I forgot to introduce you guys. Rhodes, meet Otto. Otto, meet Rhodes."

The friendly smile that Otto gave and the gesture for a handshake, forced Rhodes to smile back while shaking hands. It also gave Rhodes confidence to ask the question.

"Where did you get the wine from?" asked Rhodes.

Rhodes expected an answer from Otto, and Otto was about to open his mouth, but Lazarus the talkative, know-it-all, had to interfere.

"He is a winemaker. Or should I say he was a wine maker?" said Lazarus, followed by an irritating laughter.

Lazarus had spoken insensitively, which made Otto's face narrow. Rhodes understood that Otto was sensitive, a thing that Lazarus was not. Rhodes felt sorry looking at Otto's face.

"You said there would be four of us," said Otto.

Rhodes knew Otto was desperate to change the topic. A topic that gave Otto a miserable feeling. He also now knew the reason why Otto was ready to be part of the plan.

"Yes, he will be here soon. He must be on his way," said Lazarus, rubber necking to the far side. "There he is."

A man in steel armor, struggling through the deep snow, was approaching them.

"Is that really him?" asked Otto.

"Yep, that's him."

Rhodes knew he could not trust a traveler who showed up once every few months. A person in armor, who looked like a King's guard, approaching a thief like Rhodes, made him uncomfortable. Rhodes stood up, ready to run, in case he needed to.

"Why are you up?" asked Lazarus.

Otto was still sitting on the log.

"He is a King's guard," replied Rhodes.

"Yeah, so?" said Lazarus.

"You set it up to get me caught, didn't you?"

Lazarus laughed and said, "What?"

"Lazarus told me the other guy would be a King's guard," added Otto.

"What? Why didn't you tell me then?" asked Rhodes.

"I didn't tell you? I must've forgotten. Well, now you know," said Lazarus as he pulled Rhodes arm gently, and made him sit back on the log.

"Welcome Cicero, welcome," said Lazarus, and asked him to join them.

"Hello fellows," said Cicero, denying to sit and stood right in front of them.

"Meet Rhodes and Otto, these are the guys I told you about," said Lazarus.

"Nice to meet you," said Cicero, as he shook hands with both.

Rhodes was nervous and did not know how to react. He randomly passed the bottle of opened wine to Cicero. Lazarus handed the other bottle and said, "This one is for you to take home."

Taking a few sips, Cicero said, "Okay, let's make it quick. Let me start with the plan."

All three leaned forward, sitting on the log with

all their focus on what Cicero would say. Rhodes was curious how a King's guard had planned to break into the castle and betray the King. It would take quite a plan to enter the most guarded part of the Kingdom and steal King's belongings. Cicero took his sword from the scabbard and started sketching on the snow.

"First, we need a potato wagon," said Cicero.

"A potato wagon?" asked Rhodes.

"A wagon full of potatoes, not a wagon made of potatoes. And don't worry, I will manage that."

"What do we need it for?" asked Otto.

"Okay, no more interceptions. Let me finish talking. I will explain everything, alright?" said Cicero with a straight face.

All three nodded in approval. Rhodes was caught and beaten by King's guards on multiple occasions in the past. Being a thief and having a bad relation with King's guards, it was a strange feeling to plan stealing valuables from the castle, partnering with one of them.

"Lazarus will drive the wagon whereas you two will hide under a cover along with the potato sacks. We will have to do it just before the darkness, before my shift finishes. And we cannot be too early, because the number of guards would be high in the daytime. There might be other guards with me, but I will manage to verify the wagon for approval of entry. Lazarus will drive the wagon near the kitchen, which I will give map to, and park it along with other wagons." Cicero explained everything in detail about the plan.

"Why four?" asked Otto.

"Excuse me?" said Cicero.

"This sounds like a plan two could easily carry out. Why do you need four men in total?"

Rhodes was impressed with Otto's question. Cicero paused for a while and then replied, "More people means more eyes, things will be easier."

"Why exactly four, why not five or six then?" asked Otto.

"Do you want to be part of this plan or not?" asked Cicero, as his face turned red.

"All right guys, I think we are capable and ready for the plan," said Lazarus, deliberately interrupting the conversation.

"So, are we all in?" asked Cicero.

"I'm in," said Lazarus right away. "Rhodes?"

"What do you think is inside this chamber you are talking about?" asked Rhodes.

"I can't tell you for sure, but there is something precious. I have seen how secretly that chamber is kept."

Rhodes turned towards Otto and then looked at Cicero's face. He knew saying no now would not make sense, and this was an opportunity to be rich, forever. "Yes, I'm in," said Rhodes.

"Otto?" said Lazarus.

"In," replied Otto with a pale face.

Cicero handed the open bottle to Lazarus, and uncapped the other.

"To being rich," said Lazarus and raised the bottle, spilling some on Otto's lap. They took sips turn by turn as Rhodes pasted a forceful smile. Lazarus and Cicero had started hugging and dancing, with a bottle in the hand of each. As two of them were busy dancing drunk, Rhodes was in an awkward situation once again. He was not drunk enough to join Lazarus and Cicero. There was Otto, equally shy, sitting on the other end of the log.

"Can you believe it? When I was five, I could drink twice as much as they did and still would be less drunk," whispered Rhodes as he slid near Otto.

"I was wondering the same. Are they really drunk or just acting?" replied Otto. After a brief silence, he asked Rhodes, "Do you think we can trust them?"

"I wish I knew."

After an hour, Rhodes and Otto were still sitting on the log. Whereas, Lazarus and Cicero had walked quite far, and were having talks sitting on the snow, on the frozen lake's bank. They were shoulder to shoulder.

"Should we go?" asked Otto.

"Yeah, we should head back. Let me walk over and tell them," replied Rhodes.

Rhodes made his way through the deep snow and slowly walked towards them. As Rhodes got nearer, the talk between Lazarus and Cicero got louder. After a point, he could clearly hear what they were saying.

"How much do you think will all four of us get?" asked Lazarus.

"Not four brother, two," replied Cicero.

"Two?"

"After carrying as much of the treasure as we two can, we will lock them in," said Cicero.

"That is some plan, my brother," said Lazarus, hugging Cicero, as they both laughed.

"Hey Lazarus," yelled Rhodes before reaching

too near.

"Shush…" said Lazarus to Cicero, trying his best to act normal.

"It will be dark soon. I think we will head home now," said Rhodes.

"Yeah, sure, we will meet on the time we fixed," replied Lazarus.

"See ya' Cicero."

"See ya' rich fellow," replied Cicero.

Rhodes faked a smile and turned back. He could hear them laughing in a low volume. He was aware of the trap set by Lazarus and Cicero, but should he share it with Otto? Should he step back from the plan? After walking back to Otto, Rhodes said, "Come on, let's head on our way."

After walking a good distance from the Degerat Lake, Otto said, "Do you think it will be a success? I just want my children to have a better future."

Rhodes had given a few minutes of thoughts and could not hold the secret anymore. "I have to tell you something," he said.

"Yeah, sure."

"Earlier, while walking towards them, I heard them talk," said Rhodes.

"Yeah?"

"Their plan is to trap two of us in the castle and divide the valuables between two of them."

"What?" said Otto, as he stopped walking.

"Yes, it was a big mistake to trust someone like Lazarus in the first place."

"Wow," said Otto, and took a long breath in.

"That piece of shit and his brother Cicero had planned our funeral."

"So, we just pull out of plan?" asked Otto, as

they started walking again.

"There are two options, either pull out of plan, or,"

"Or what?"

"Or we double cross them and plan their funeral instead," said Rhodes.

"I don't know man, sounds too dangerous."

"Look, Otto, my friend. I have known you for only a couple of hours, but I know what kind of person you are. Your family matters the most to you and you want a better future for you children. You want your wife to be happy. You are a nice guy, I get it. But you need this money. And so do I. We need to teach these asses a lesson too."

"What do you do for a living?" asked Otto abruptly.

"What?" said Rhodes.

"What do you do for a living? It is a simple question."

"Well…" Rhodes scratched his head.

"You are a thief, Lazarus told me."

"You can call me that," he said with a pity face.

"So you want me to ditch two frauds and trust a thief?" said Otto. Rhodes was out of words. Otto was right, and Rhodes could think of nothing to defend himself. Although Rhodes was honest and he knew Otto was a nice guy, he was in a difficult situation. "So can you explain the plan in detail?" added Otto.

"The plan?"

"The plan to double cross those moppets."

Rhodes smiled, and so did Otto.

CHAPTER 8

When the ass opened its eyes, the sun was just above the horizon. The fire had gone off, Otto and Rhodes were lying on each side of the ass. After taking a few steps ahead, the ass felt pain on its leg. There was a wound from the other night's accident.

"Rhodes, wake up," said Otto, stretching, adjusting his back.

Rhodes pushed Otto in his sleep before coming back to sense. Otto froze in surprise. "I'm sorry, I do this when someone wakes me up this way," said Rhodes.

"It's fine. We need to get on our way."

They got ready and walked ahead. The ass was in pain, but not enough to stop it from walking. Otto and Rhodes could do something about the wound, but they did not seem to notice. After walking for a while, the ass changed the rhythm of its walk. Not because it was in pain and couldn't walk normally anymore, but because it wanted others to notice.

"What is wrong with the ass?" asked Rhodes.

"I don't know, it's walking funny," replied Otto.

"Something is wrong with its leg."

After a quick scan, Otto found out about the wound. "There is a wound on its leg."

"We are in the middle of nowhere, we can't do anything about it." They took the vessels off the ass and each carried one.

"Maybe we'll find something on the next settlement."

They kept walking, and the ass was now in trouble. It had changed the walking style to make them notice the wound, but keeping up for long tired the ass. The fake walk was now a headache for the ass. After walking for few hours they finally reached a settlement. There were only few structures, but there were people in good number.

"Look, an apothecary," said Rhodes.

Putting down the vessel, Otto smiled and said, "We will be fixing your leg now, is that alright Snaky." He caressed the ass.

Rhodes laughed and said, "Snaky?"

"Yes, a nickname for the ass."

"But, why Snaky?"

"Look at the locket it's wearing, it has a snake on it,"

Rhodes focused on the locket and said, "I don't see a head or a tail."

"Well, it has the shape of a snake."

Rhodes laughed again and replied, "Snaky it is then."

They tied the ass on a wooden post just outside the apothecary and entered carrying the vessels. The ass looked around wondering where would they eat the next meal. There was a bakery on the other side of the road. On the outside, a dog had a loaf of bread in its mouth. A man with torn clothes and covered in dirt was trying its best to snatch the bread off the dog's mouth.

"Come on, Snaky, we are going in," said Otto, as he came out of the apothecary.

He untied the ass and took it inside. There was Rhodes and a man inside waiting for the ass. There was a wooden shelf as high as the wall itself and on all four sides. They were full of transparent bottles filled with powders and liquids in distinct colors.

"Let me prepare the mix," said the man, and took few bottles from the shelf. He took a pinch from every bottle and put them on the tiny crusher made of stone.

"Did you buy those vessels from the nearby market?" asked the man, as he continued crushing the mix.

Otto and Rhodes looked at each other. They wondered why the man asked about the vessels out of nowhere.

"No, we bought it in a shop near the King's castle," replied Otto.

The man stopped crushing and froze for a brief and said, "Near the castle?"

"Yes, why?" asked Otto.

"I thought they made these kinds of vessels only in Mic Oras."

The talk about vessels made Rhodes uncomfortable. It could have been dangerous. He had to change the topic.

"Who is that man?" asked Rhodes, pointing to a painting that hung on one of the shelves.

"My father."

"Is that the King on his side?" asked Otto.

"Yes, my father worked in the castle, and one time, the King ordered the painter to paint him along with my father."

The way the man talked clarified that his father was dead. The man's link to the King and the castle had worried Otto and Rhodes.

"You know what people used to say about my father? They used to say, he had so much knowledge about the mixes, he could do miracles. He could make stones talk if he wanted."

"What happened to him?" asked Otto.

"He was murdered in the castle," said the man as his eyes turned red and his voice turned shaky. The sudden change in the mood of the man frightened Otto and Rhodes. They froze and listened. "They say he fell from one of the towers, but I'm sure he was murdered."

Rhodes could not wait to exit the apothecary. He said, "Sir, how long will it take for the mix to be ready?"

"It's about ready. And you can call me Marcus Junior."

Marcus Junior approached the ass. "Why are its eyes wet," asked Rhodes as he noticed teardrops on its eyes.

"It could be the pain from the wound," replied Marcus Junior. He gently applied the mix in the wound. "This should do."

Rhodes reached deep into his pocket to grab monedas. "It's fine, I cannot take money for spreading humanity."

"But you make mixes for living. How do you even afford your expenses?" asked Otto.

Marcus Junior laughed and replied, "Don't you worry about it, my friend."

"You are a good man."

"Make sure the ass does not carry much weights until the wound heels."

Rhodes and Otto exited the apothecary along with the ass. They carried one vessel each as the ass walked with eyes full of tears.

"Snaky is in genuine pain, I think," said Rhodes.

"I thought animals screamed and bit others while in discomfort. This is sobbing in silence," said Otto.

"Maybe it is not crying, could it be something else?"

"Maybe it's hungry."

"Ass crying with tears because it's hungry? Doesn't sound right. But I am hungry, though."

"Should we find a bakery?"

"Let's find a place that has Cheese with mushroom and nuts, Snaky's favorite."

They found a place to eat. They ordered Cheese with mushroom and nuts but the place was out of mushroom. As they waited for the food to come, Rhodes started the conversation. "What do you think about these vessels?"

"What do you mean?" asked Otto.

"Do you think these are some unusual vessels, is there anything special about these?"

Otto turned to either side and whispered, "Cicero and Lazarus risked everything for the plan. If these vessels do not sell for good money, things don't make sense. It has to be valuable."

The ass that had its tongue out all the time and made a funny face showing two of its front teeth was on the floor with mouth closed and eyes full of tears. It stared a stone on the floor as if it was lost in thoughts. Rhodes and Otto wanted to help but did not know what was wrong with it.

"The food is here, Snaky, your favorite," said Otto as it took the plate and placed it near to it. The ass turned the other way. Rhodes and Otto tried their best, but the ass did not eat.

"Could it be because there is no mushroom in it?" asked Rhodes.

"I don't think that's it."

"Hey, what are you doing, that plate is for humans to eat. Don't take it near that filthy animal," yelled the owner of the place.

Rhodes and Otto ate, but the ass did not. They got on their way back again.

"Hey, look, it's walking just fine, it's not the wound," whispered Rhodes to Otto.

"That's right. Something else is bothering it."

"It's not hunger, it's not wound. Don't tell me it is homesick."

They walked for hours. Rhodes and Otto carried the vessels until their hand no longer were capable. The ass was walking fine, so they tied the vessels onto its back. Few hours of walk took them into a narrow jungle in the middle of the forest with no human activities around.

"We are walking through this jungle forever and it does not seem to end anytime soon," said Otto.

"It's strange. We must have taken a wrong turn. This cannot be the way."

"Should we take a rest? We have been walking since forever."

Otto crashed on a pile of snow as he would on the bed. Rhodes sat on a log nearby.

"What are we doing?" said Rhodes.

"What?"

"What are we doing? You are away from your children and pregnant wife, walking with an ass and a thief with couple of vessels, which I don't think has any value."

"You don't know that."

"I know."

"What are you so depressed about?" asked Otto.

Suddenly, Rhodes said, standing upright, "Did you hear that?"

"Hear what?"

Rhodes shushed Otto as they stood all ears.

"Grab the ass' lead," said Rhodes, and walked into the dense jungle with trees covered in snow. Lights barely passed through the canopy.

"Slow down Rhodes," said Otto struggling to follow Rhodes with the ass on a thick vegetation with knee deep snow.

"Help."

"Rhodes, the sound came from the right," yelled Otto from behind.

Otto lost Rhodes visually. He shouted Rhodes' name and followed his track.

"Here," yelled Rhodes.

When Otto finally reached there, he saw Rhodes on his knees next to a small girl. Her face was covered in dirt and she had messy hair. Her leg was tied to a log with a thick rope.

"She was just here all alone, tied to the log?" asked Otto.

"Yes, now help me untie her."

Otto kneeled down to help Rhodes. "This is an easy loop, I'm surprised you haven't got it open yet," said Otto.

"I'm not good with knots." The looks Otto gave Rhodes fed him a certain urge to defend himself. He added, "I know, I know, I'm a thief that's not good with knots. Now stop judging."

Otto smiled, which did not last for long as he realized something. "We are untying knot of a rope tied to a girl's leg in the middle of a ghostly jungle. A knot that's easy to open," whispered Otto.

After Otto untied the rope, Rhodes asked the girl softly, "What's your name? Who did this to you?"

The girl that was silent the whole time stood and screamed in almost ultrasonic sound. The deep, sharp sound forced Rhodes and Otto to cover their ears.

"Well, well, who do we have here," said a man appearing from the dark jungle. He had a freshly broken branch of a pine tree that he held on his shoulder. It had human limbs tied with the help of a thin string with blood still dripping from a few. There were three other men with him. Two of them had bow and arrow aimed at Rhodes and Otto. As the man walked near, the smell and visual of the limbs got an effect on them. Otto could not hold the vomit anymore.

"Please tell me those are animal limbs," whispered Otto, shaking.

"Those are not animal limbs, and we are in a huge trouble," replied Rhodes, whispering.

"So, we got ourselves a first timer," said the man looking at Otto. He then stretched his hands, getting the tied limbs near Otto's face. He grabbed his stomach in pain and continued vomiting.

"We want no trouble, just let us go," said Otto, while on the floor, on his knees.

"Yeah, sure, why not," replied the man mockingly. "Let's free all the chickens, let's free all the goats," added the man, followed by a laughter.

"What?" said Otto.

"We are their food Otto, just look at them," whispered Rhodes.

CHAPTER 9

"Antonius, why is that donkey on the loose?" asked the King.

"It is not a donkey, your majesty, it is an ass."

"Fascinating, do they look the same? Is it the size?"

"Yes, your majesty, they look the same. It's a young one, so it's small."

"How do you know it's an ass and not a donkey?"

"Domesticated asses are called donkey. It is in the wild, so it is an ass, your majesty."

"Come here, small thing," said the King, as he bent on his knees and offered his hands. The little ass walked to the King, wiggling its tail. "Look at you, aren't you cute," said the King, taking the baby ass in his arms. "Little Octavius will now have a friend too," added the King, as Antonius smiled back.

The King woke up to the dream. The ass was right in front of him, wiggling its tail.

"Look how much you've grown. I just dreamt of the day I found you in the jungle, you were so little," said the King, caressing the ass.

Octavius entered the King's chamber. "Oh, I'm sorry your majesty, I just came to take the ass with me."

"Look, your friend is here," said the King to the ass. Octavius gestured with his hands and the ass followed him, as they walked towards the exit. "Octavius," said the king.

"Yes, your majesty."

"If you see Marcus, send him here."

"I saw him just before coming here, I will pass the message, your majesty."

In the north tower of the castle, The General was waiting for Marcus.

"Come my friend," said General as he closed the door. "I hope you brought, what I asked for."

"This is wrong, very wrong, General," said Marcus, with a tight throat.

"You don't even know what I'm going to do with it, how do you know it's wrong?" said the General, with a soft smile.

"You threatened to kill my family, and you asked for it to be a secret. It cannot be for anything good, can it?"

"You are a smart man, Marcus. I can tell you what I am going to do with it, but after telling you, I will have to kill you."

"I don't care, I did this to save my family."

"I know Marcus, and that is what smart men do. They die for good of others."

"And it's not that hard to figure, you know. There are not many things you would do with the mixes," said Marcus.

"Is that so?"

"Yes, I know. You will gulp the mix and also trick the King to do the same."

"Well, well, you do know then."

"It is wrong, General. Please think thoroughly before you do anything stupid."

"Don't you worry about it, Marcus. Everything is thought of."

The King sat on the wooden chair, made specially to comfort his troubling back. The rare glance of sunlight gave warmth to his chilly red skin, as he sat on the back garden of the castle, between the piles of snow. He liked the garden green and snow free, but the recent weather was opposite to his likings. There were teapot and cups on the table, on his side, but he was too lazy to even take a sip.

"General, what are you up to," yelled the King when he saw the General racing towards the gate.

General walked to the King and bowed, "Your majesty."

"Where were you rushing to?" asked the King.

"I was just…"

"Come join me for the tea," said the King, interrupting.

"Sure, your majesty." General sat and poured a cup of tea.

They both had conversation watching Octavius play with the ass. "Who would have thought an ass would become a man's best friend," said the King, followed by a laughter. General smiled as he took a sip from the cup.

"Your majesty, there was something I needed to show you," said the General in sweetest tone.

"Yeah, sure, what is it?"

"It is the new weapon Marcus helped us develop."

"Marcus helped to develop a weapon?" asked the King, with his eyebrows raised.

"Yes, your majesty."

"Is there anything that man can't do?" said the King, followed by a smile, as he rested his back on the chair, closing his eyes.

"We need your approval for its deployment."

"Sure, sure, is it fine we do that after a while," the King closed his eyes, with his face up to the sun and his head rested on the back of the seat.

"Sure, your majesty. It's in the dungeon."

"In the dungeon? You want me to walk up to the dungeon with this back?" said the King, as he opened one of his eyes and gave a side look to the General.

"We would bring it here, but it's too big and heavy. We can still do that, but it will take a few days."

"It's fine General, let's go," said the King, as he leaned forward with his hands on the hand-rest of the chair and stood up.

The King walked towards the Dungeon with General. When the ass saw the King walk, it ran towards him and walked along. "How long till the summer, General. I am sick of these blizzards and skin freezing cold," said the King as he patted the head of the ass.

"Just a few months more, your majesty."

After a long walk, they finally reached the Dungeon. The King was busy catching breath as he sat on a stone, carved in the shape of a seat. "Do you keep water or something to drink around here?" asked the King.

"Yes we do, your majesty," said the General, as he walked to a dark chamber on the far side. The King sat there waiting as he caressed the ass.

"Here your majesty," said the General, as he handed a goblet to the King, while he kept one to himself. The King finished the water in a single go and said, "It tastes funny, doesn't it?"

The General was about to drink as well, but the ass bit him gently on the leg. General spilled the water on the floor, and he jumped, pulling his leg. The King laughed and said, "Don't worry General, he does that sometimes. A bite without teeth." The ass licked the spilled water. "It was thirsty from the walk too, hah." The General froze with his eyes wide open. "So where is this weapon Marcus helped to build?" asked the King.

The General slowly walked to another chamber next to the previous one. He stayed there for a while before walking back to the King. "Your majesty, the weapon is not here. Maybe they shifted it to somewhere else."

"Don't you joke with me, General. Don't tell me you seriously made me walk all this way for bloody nothing."

CHAPTER 10

In the middle of the jungle, with trees covered white on snow, there was a small area of clear ground. There was a bonfire blazing in the middle, lighting up the whole of the surrounding. Rhodes and Otto were tied to a log with their hands behind them. They sat on the snow with their legs forward, facing the fire. The ass was tied to a tree near them. They were surrounded by people with face full of dirt and hair tangled, as if they had never bathed their entire life. They had cut deer skin into different shapes, which they wore to save themselves from the cold. One of them had an unusual appearance. He had a bracelet on his wrist, made of bones of babies, and wore a chain on his neck full of fingers, with blood still dripping from them. He turned towards the other Salbat and said in a calm voice, contrary to his appearance, "Are we having soup tonight?"

"Soup? What do you mean, Lord Vinicius?" said Picaro.

"They are too skinny for a steak, aren't they, Picaro? Where did you find them?"

"We used the girl to drive them towards the woods, the old way, Lord Vinicius."

Vinicius walked towards Rhodes and Otto, got a feel of the meat on their leg and arms, and said, "Huh, well, better than nothing, I guess."

Otto and Rhodes turned towards each other, shaking. The words of Vinicius confused Picaro. "Lord Vinicius, so do we cook them like a soup or…"

"Oh Picaro, for god's sake. I was just kidding, sizzle them the regular way."

Picaro smiled and signaled a tall, muscular man, who was holding a Garden fork as tall as himself.

"How are they going to chop us with a garden fork?" said Rhodes, sobbing.

Otto could hold no more and started crying his hearts out. "He will poke us to death and tear our limbs, won't he? I don't want to die, Rhodes, please do something."

A distant sound of horses and clang of metal grabbed attention of everyone. "Is it time for dinner yet?" said a man with armor of King's guard on.

There were a good number of other King's guards behind him on horses.

"Come General, come. It definitely is time for dinner, but sadly you don't eat what we do."

Rhodes and Otto froze in silence as they saw General and an entire unit of King's guard having a pleasant talk with the Salbats, right in front of their eyes. The man that approached them, to tear them into dinner, stood there smiling as he watched Vinicius talk to the General.

"Yeah, sadly I don't. Try cooking goat for a dinner sometimes," said the General.

"Well, we got no goat. Does a donkey work?"

"A donkey?"

"Yes, Picaro found a donkey along with these men today," said Vinicius, extending his arms towards the corner where Rhodes, Otto and the Donkey were tied.

General walked towards the ass. There were two familiar looking vessels alongside the ass.

"This is not a donkey, it's bloody ass from the castle, for god's sake," said the General, as his voice turned sharper and volume went up.

"What?" said Vinicius, as his face turned colorless.

"The King has sent guards in every corner of the kingdom looking for this ass and probably these vessels too. Get rid of them as soon as possible. You could be in a big trouble already."

"Already?"

"Yes, there are people in the Castle who can track a deer in a blizzard, It's only a matter of time before they visit this little camp of yours."

"No problem General. We can eat the men, break and bury the vessels and kill the donkey. We can then cut it into pieces and feed the wolves. The jungle is full of hungry wolves," said Vinicius in a soft and calm voice.

"It's not that easy, you idiot, they can track you. Possibly you got me into trouble as well."

"Now, mind your words, General. You maybe General of the castle, but here, you are just a guest. A guest, as long as we treat you as a guest."

"Is that so?" said the General, with raised eyebrows.

"Yes, that's it," said Vinicius, staring right into the General's eye.

General gave a soft smile, then he drew his sword from the scabbard and cut through the front of Vinicius' stomach. Every organ inside of him slid out and fell out of his stomach onto the floor, right in front of his eyes.

Every Salbat that surrounded the bonfire screamed in fear, as they could not believe their eyes.

"Shut up," screamed the General. Everybody backed off and whimpered as Vinicius laid on the snowy ground that had turned red, grabbing his organs, gasping his last breaths.

"Mamma, I'm hungry," said a little girl to her mother. She shushed her kid.

"Didn't you hear her? She is hungry. Give her something to eat, for god's sake," said the General.

The man with the garden fork stabbed in the groin of Rhodes a few times. He then tore the leg messily off his body. The scream of Rhodes from the pain was so loud, it got General worried that someone could hear him.

"What the fuck are you doing?" yelled the General.

The man with the fork stuffed Rhodes mouth with snow. He then tied the wound with the torn piece of pant that came along with the torn limb. Blood had already flooded, turning cold snow around him steamy red. Otto watched in silence as Rhodes screamed in pain.

"Now every one of you do as I say," yelled the General, taking a slow walk around the bonfire. "Every one of you is in trouble. King's men could be here any minute and they are not as friendly as we are. They don't even know you guys exist. This could be the end of Salbats, so listen to what I say and also, only do as I say."

The man who tore Rhodes' leg off his body used the garden fork to hold the leg near the fire. Rhodes and Otto watched as the leg started sizzling right in front of their eyes.

"The little girl is hungry. It will take hours for the leg to cook that way, for god's sake."

"Why don't you cook them yourself, then," said the man with fork.

General gave the signal with his hand. A few guards walked towards the man and stabbed their swords into the big man's chest. He drowned on his own blood and kneeled down just before collapsing on the ground.

"Feed the young ones. Then, each one of you will follow me into the woods," yelled the General. The crowd listened quietly but could barely trust the General, at least after killing two of their men. One being their trusted leader.

CHAPTER 11

Rhodes screamed for a while before going unconscious, as Otto tied him on the back of the ass and ran away from the jungle. It was only a matter of time before General and his men returned and found them missing. In the darkness, with the help of the moonlight, they ran back through the way they came. Otto was aware if he took Rhodes to the apothecary on time, he would be patched up and perhaps his life would be saved.

"Hang on, buddy," said Otto to the unconscious Rhodes. Otto supported Rhodes on the back of the ass to stop him from falling.

The sound of people screaming in a distance frightened Otto. The massacre of Salbats going on in the jungle, echoed. The road which previously led them towards the jungle in a few hours, felt much longer this time, even though Otto and the ass ran as fast as they could. When they finally reached the apothecary, they found the door closed. Otto knocked on the door a few times.

"Go away, we are closed," said someone from inside.

"It's an emergency, please," said Otto quietly.

"Come tomorrow."

"Please, we are the ones from earlier today, it's an emergency," said Otto in a shaky voice.

Candle light glowed inside, as Otto could see reflections under the door. The door slowly opened to the halfway. When the light of the candle from inside made the unconscious Rhodes, soaked in blood, visible, Marcus Junior gestured Otto to get inside. A naked woman, covered in a bedsheet, stood stunned in the corner.

"What happened, oh my god," said Marcus Junior, closing the door.

"The Salbats, they did this, please do something," said Otto, crying.

"The Salbats? They exist for real?" said Marcus Junior, as his eyes widened. After freezing for a few seconds, he added, "Let me grab a few things."

"We don't have time, people are after us. Me and the ass need to leave right now."

"Who are after you?"

"I will explain later, just take care of him. And

the King's guards might make a visit, so hide him somewhere."

"But…"

"Please Marcus, I need to leave," said Otto, and grabbed the lead of the ass, and exited the apothecary.

It was not safe for Otto and the ass to take the regular way back, so they travelled through the hills and jungles. With Rhodes in safe hands, Otto could think wisely for once. He had to walk back to the castle and tell everything to the King. It would be in the best interest of everyone. After walking through the wilderness in the darkness for hours, he could not compress the thoughts inside of him anymore. They sat on a giant stone in a hill, watching the four towers of the castle shine with the help of huge fire torches in a distance.

"I will do everything I can, to return you back to the King," said Otto, with a smile, caressing the ass. "All I wanted was a good life for my wife and kids. Is that a bad thing? From what I witnessed earlier, I am far from being bad. I know I played a part in stealing you and the vessels, but it did no harm to any innocent souls." The ass looked into Otto's eyes while he spoke his hearts out. The ass then slept with its head on Otto's lap.

They woke up to the sound of birds and chirping insects of the jungle. It was still dark, but the sun would be up in a few hours. They had slept hugging each other, keeping each other warm.

"Come on, we need to go now," said Otto, as he took the lead.

They walked up and down hills, and walked through the jungle, before they came across a small river. The river was half frozen, and the water was freezing cold. The ass was so thirsty that it did not care how cold the water was. It drank as much as it could.

"We are not that far now. Not much before you and I part. I will definitely miss you," said Otto, giving a soft smile. "I have gone crazy haven't I? Have been having a one-way conversation for a while now."

With every step, they were closing on to the castle. The sun had come up over the horizon and Otto could hear the human activities nearby.

"We are almost there. There are no more ways through the jungle. We have to take the road now," said Otto to the ass.

They walked out to the road and approached the Castle's gate. guards on the front of the castle could see Otto grabbing the lead of the ass and walking towards the castle.

"Octavius, call the King. Tell him a man with an ass is approaching the castle," said Antonius, as he rushed down from the castle tower towards the gate.

When Antonius reached the gate, Otto was lying

flat on the ground in front of the gate with an arrow on the back of his head. The ass stood by Otto's body with tear drops dripping from its eyes.

"Now, that's what I call a bull's eye," said the General, as he walked towards the castle gate from behind, with a bow in his hand. A few guards approached on a horse from behind, following the General.

The King came running from inside the castle, and hugged the ass. "Oh, Stephen, thank god you're alright."

"Your majesty," said the General, as he bowed in front of the King. The ass stared at the General with eyes full of tears.

The King rushed inside the castle with the ass. He took the ass to his chamber and locked the door.

"Your majesty, are you alright? What exactly happened? Tell me everything," said the King to the ass.

"Lock the General in the chamber and prepare the gallows. The General will be hanged tonight," replied the ass.

"Hang the General? Are you sure, your majesty?" asked the King.

"Yes Stephen, I will explain everything later," said the ass, then climbed the King's bed and went to sleep.

CPSIA information can be obtained
at www.ICGtesting.com
Printed in the USA
LVHW050157200922
728811LV00005B/222

9 798564 982085